PETER and the WOLF

To Florence and C.F.

PETER and the WOLF

Retold and Illustrated by
ROBERT SARGENT

Lancelot Press

There weren't many animals on the farm where Peter lived, because Peter's grandfather just couldn't take care of them like he used to. They had a cow and a horse, who lived in the barn, and a few chicks. There weren't any pigs, because Peter's grandfather said it took too long to fatten a pig and too much care to keep one clean. So the chicks lived in the pig pens.

There was a duck who just wouldn't live in any one place. She would strut up and down the yard and back and forth to the pond as if she owned the whole meadow! So Peter couldn't really tell exactly where she lived.

And there was the cat, of course. She lived in the house. She spent most of the time with Peter's grandmother and only came out when the grass was dry to catch bugs and beetles and to chase butterflies in the evening sunset.

Peter's grandfather was an old sea captain and since Peter had come to live with his grandmother and grandfather, he had been told hundreds of stories about the great and dangerous sea and about far off places where the strangest things happened.

When Peter lay awake at night, watching the shadows glide across his bedroom walls, he would imagine he was a captain standing on a rolling deck with the sails blowing high on the mast.

Peter made up his mind that his grandfather must have been one of the bravest sailors that ever was. And he made up his mind that he wasn't going to be afraid of anything either.

That was just about the only trouble with the countryside. It was too peaceful! Nothing exciting ever happened that you could tell anyone about. How could you know how brave you were if nothing ever happened?

In the afternoons, when the sunshine came into the backyard in soft patterns through the trees, Peter's grandfather would sit out by the washtub and whittle and carve sailing ships.

Peter would either go over by the fence under the hollyhocks to build a city made of fresh wood chips, or stay up by the shed and swing in the breezes that blew in off the meadow.

If Peter wanted to sail his own boats down at the pond, his grandfather would go along with him. But he was never to go there alone.

The forest nearby had many wild animals in it. Peter's grandfather said that any one of them might stray out for a drink at the pond and, seeing Peter, could change his mind and decide to have dinner instead.

Early in the mornings, of all the places on the farm, Peter liked the meadow best.

When the spider webs were still stretched across the violets, and the newest blossoms were bursting forth, Peter would step just outside the gate to smell the freshness of the new day. The meadow, with all her red and yellow and blue flowers, was like a great bouquet waking up to the sun. Peter, the crickets, a few earthworms, and some birds were happiest there.

Of course the earthworms and the crickets had to keep a lookout for the birds, and Peter had to keep a lookout for his grandfather.

One morning, when Peter had stepped outside to have a new look at the meadow, the duck waddled out through the open gate and headed down to the pond for her morning swim. She had just reached the water's edge when a little bird, who usually nested in the shed above Peter's swing, got into a terrible argument with her!

The duck quacked and quacked and was very annoyed with the little bird. The little bird hopped up and down on the shore in a frenzy of temper!

Then Peter saw the cat silently creeping through
the long blades of grass.

Her eyes glowed in the sunlight
as she studied the duck and the bird.

Obviously they were unaware of their visitor!

Peter called out to the bird just in time! Swiftly she flew up into the tree. The duck quacked in alarm and swam as fast as she could to the middle of the pond, out of the cat's reach.

And how she quacked at the cat!

But the cat wasn't interested in the duck—she was busy watching the bird and trying to decide if she should climb the tree after it.

Just as the cat arrived at the base of the tree and was about to climb it, Peter's grandfather stormed out of the open gate with scolding words for Peter and a strong warning about the wolves in the forest.

He took Peter's hand tightly and led him back into the yard, locking the gate after them.

Peter's grandfather then went to repair a hayfork in the shed, and Peter, not feeling the least bit nervous after his grandfather's warning, returned to the gate to watch the cat and the bird.

Just then a great, grey wolf came out of the bushes at the edge of the forest!

In a flash, the cat dashed up the tree to safety.

But the duck became so frightened that she forgot she was already in the safest place of all, and without realizing it, she spluttered and splashed herself completely out of the pond! She tried to waddle through the long grass, but the wolf leaped forward and—with a great gnashing of teeth—swallowed her!

Perched nervously on the opposite branch from the cat, the little bird nearly swallowed her tongue out of sheer fright when the wolf swallowed the duck!

The wolf, not satisfied with his duck dinner, looked up greedily at the cat and the bird.

Peter suddenly had an idea! He ran to the shed and pulled a rope down off the wall. He did it so skillfully that his grandfather never even noticed that he had been there.

Then Peter ran to the stone wall near the fence and pulled himself up into the tree by grabbing the end of a low branch.

While Peter tied a lasso in the end of the rope, the bird flew down around the head of the wolf and circled about his ears, keeping him busy.

The wolf jumped back and forth trying to catch the bird in his jaws, and never noticed what was happening in the tree.

Then Peter dropped the rope down near the wolf, and after only two tries, he caught the wolf's tail and pulled with all his might! Then Peter quickly tied the rope to the tree branch. The wolf leaped furiously into the air when he felt the rope, but his leaping about only made the rope grow tighter!

Suddenly a band of hunters came out of the forest. They had been looking for the wolf all morning and were ready to shoot him on sight.

Peter waved to them from the tree.

"We've caught the wolf!" he cried. "We've caught the wolf!"

The hunters came across the meadow quickly, and with another strong rope, they tied the wolf's jaws closed.

"Don't kill him!" cried Peter. "Let's take him to the zoo!"

So that afternoon, after Peter's grandmother had served the hunters lunch and coffee in the yard, and after Peter's grandfather had given Peter another strong warning about having anything at all to do with wolves, they all marched over the hill and into the village, to the zoo.

They were all proud of their catch—but Peter, the bird, and the cat were the proudest of all!